THE SCOURGE OF THE DINNER LADIES

Caroline Crisp overhears the dinner ladies plotting a new job but she is soon spotted eavesdropping. Before she knows it, she's been kidnapped, for use as a 'snatcher' to help the Granny Fang Gang with their thieving!

Can Craig Vague and Wayne Drain save Caroline from her fate?

)

**Also by the same author,
and available in Knight Books:**

THE HEADMASTER WENT SPLAT!

The Scourge of the Dinner Ladies

David Tinkler

Illustrated by David McKee

KNIGHT BOOKS
Hodder and Stoughton

First published in Great Britain in 1987
by Anderson Press Limited

Knight edition 1989
Fifth impression 1990

British Library C.I.P.

Tinkler, David
The scourge of the dinner ladies
I. Title
823'.914[J]

ISBN 0 340 50166 9

Printed and bound in Great Britain for
Hodder and Stoughton Paper-
backs, a division of Hodder and
Stoughton Ltd., Mill Road, Dunton
Green, Sevenoaks, Kent TN13 2YA.
(Editorial Office: 47 Bedford Square,
London WC1B 3DP) by Cox & Wyman
Ltd., Reading, Berks.

Chomp. Chomp. Burp. Slurp.

This was the noise of dinner time at the Littlesprat Primary School. Nobody dared to talk. No. The children just sat there chomping and slurping and trying not to clatter their knives and forks.

There was a girl called Caroline Crisp in there chomping with the rest; I suppose you'd call her a girl even though she looked like a swarm of freckles with red hair on top! It was as if a swarm of freckles had escaped from a freckle farm and swooped on Caroline Crisp. A pair of inquisitive, green eyes peered out from the freckles; they looked this way and that.

'Why is everyone so quiet?' she whispered to the boy sitting next to her. This boy was Craig Vague; he was a bit dreamy. Craig looked at Caroline in a startled, surprised sort of way. She was a new girl, so he felt he'd better reply even though it was very, very dangerous.

'What?' he hissed.

'What do you mean "what"?' replied the freckled girl with a frown. 'Are you deaf or something?'

A dinner lady suddenly appeared behind them. 'Who was that?' she yelled. 'Who was whispering? Craig—it was you!'

'No I ....'

'DON'T YOU SAY NO TO ME, YOUNG MAN—

YOU WAS WHISPERING!'

'I'm sorry, Mrs Sludge.'

'WHO WAS YOU WHISPERING WITH? WAS IT YOU?' she bellowed, glaring at Caroline. Caroline's freckles seemed to glow as if they'd been lit up from behind. This was because she'd gone terribly pale which made the freckles stand out.

'N—no . . .' she stammered.

'OH YES IT WAS. IT WAS YOU, YOUNG LADY!'

'I—I didn't know.'

'DIDN'T KNOW WHAT?'

'That you aren't allowed to talk or whisper. At my old school you could talk.'

'WELL, THIS ISN'T YOUR OLD SCHOOL, IS IT?'

'No.'

Mrs Sludge peered about to see if anyone was going to make a noise. Wayne Drain made a noise, up at the other end. He belched. The children sniggered; they just couldn't help it.

'WAYNE DRAIN, WAS THAT YOU?'

'Was that me doing what?' asked Wayne looking innocent.

'BELCHING!'

'I think,' replied Wayne calmly, 'that it was Miss Thrasher!'

The children sniggered even more; Miss Thrasher was the Head Teacher. Wayne Drain was extra good at

being cheeky. If there had been cups and prizes for cheek and mischief, young Wayne would have got the lot.

Mrs Sludge was the roughest, toughest dinner lady that there has ever been, which is saying a lot. She glared with fierce eyes at the cheeky boy, opened her mouth and yelled: 'SHUT UP! DON'T DO IT NO MORE—OR I'LL HIT YER WIV ME LADLE!'

She had this huge ladle for ladling out soup and stew and custard (sometimes all at once to save time). Mrs Sludge began to trudge towards Wayne waving her ladle menacingly. Soon he felt it wafting over his hair. Then he heard Mrs Sludge roaring in his ear and smelt her evil breath. 'I got my eye on you, my boy. You're a trouble maker, you are!'

She stomped off glaring at the children and nodding at the other dinner ladies as if to say, 'That's how to deal with trouble!'

THRPP!

'Who did that?'

No one answered. There was a lot of sniggering and chortling and nudging, but no one owned up.

'Wayne Drain, was that you?'

'Was that me doing what?' asked Wayne with his special hurt, baffled, innocent look.

'You know what—it *was* you, wasn't it?'

'What was?'

Rage rippled through Mrs Sludge's big body; her cross, angry face went tomato red. She gripped her

8

ladle with both hands and *bent* it in her temper till it looked like a huge hair-grip.

'Now look what you've gone and made me do!' she roared.

Nobody moved. Everyone was quiet. Then somebody spoke. A girl.

'No, he didn't,' gulped this girl's voice bravely. 'No one made you bend it. You just did it by yourself.'

That was Caroline Crisp's view on the matter. That's what she thought about it all.

The children had been quiet before but now they were extra silent. It was as if they were toy children sitting there not breathing or moving. What's going to happen? That's what those extra-silent children were wondering.

2

Here is a very simple question: do you think Mrs Sludge could win a beauty contest? The answer is Yes—but it would have to be a special beauty contest for people who look like wart-hogs. As I expect you realise, only the male wart-hog has tusks; the females seem to get along without them, which was just as well for Caroline Crisp.

Mrs Sludge started to trudge.

Trudge. Trudge. Trudge. That was her heavy feet plodding along. She had grabbed a steaming jug of custard. Being a dinner lady she was especially good at pouring hot custard over things and that's what she was going to do to Caroline Crisp. It was old Batty who stopped her. Batty was the maddest of the dinner ladies—the one who talked to herself and shrieked out laughing for no reason. Batty was always making batter, which was one of the reasons for her name. The other reason was that she was bats. But only a bit: she knew that Mrs Sludge would get into trouble for pouring a jug of hot custard over one of the children. It would be considered wasteful. So she dashed up behind the trudging Sludge and grabbed her by the sleeve—the white sleeve of her dinner-lady coat. 'Don't do it, Sludge, or Miss Thrasher will do her nut!'

'So what?' snapped the Sludge.

'And Granny Fang!' said Batty. 'Granny wouldn't like it. She might . . . .'

Batty stopped talking out loud because she realised that they were right behind Craig Vague and she didn't want him to hear what she was going to say next. Then she put her lips very, very close to Mrs Sludge's earhole and told her what Granny Fang might do. The Sludge listened; then she turned slowly round, ready to trudge back and put the custard down nice and calmly.

Craig had turned his head slowly as soon as he'd heard little Batty whispering about Mrs Fang, the school cook. Now his eyes were open wide and his mouth was open too; he'd seen something amazing: a tattoo. Yes, a tattoo on Mrs Sludge's arm where Batty had pulled the sleeve back. It said:

GRANNY FANG AND
HER ALL GIRL
GANG

Craig's wide eyes watched as Mrs Sludge trudged back to the serving hatch and plonked down the steaming jug of custard. She looked at it with a sigh, then glared at Caroline Crisp.

'Right!' she roared. 'You can stay behind after dinner and do the clearing up!'

'I don't think they're really dinner ladies,' Craig hissed as the two boys wandered back to their class-room after dinner. 'I saw this tattoo on Mrs Sludge's arm! *Granny Fang*, it said, *Granny Fang and her all girl gang!'*

'Don't be daft!' laughed Wayne.

But maybe Craig wasn't so daft. If Wayne had been standing sneakily next to the open serving hatch listening to what Caroline Crisp was listening to, I think he'd have changed his mind.

She'd finished loading up the trolley and was supposed to be on her way back to the classroom. But she just could not resist sneaking up to that hatch and peeping through to look at those amazing, fiend-like dinner ladies.

Trudge. Trudge. Trudge. That was the trudge of the Sludge as she went back to the kitchen pushing the trolley piled high with yucky-mucky dinner plates.

Cackle. Cackle. Swig. Swig. Puff. Puff. The rest of the dinner ladies cackled merrily as they played cards, boozed and puffed at their pipes. They were happy because a bad brat had been forced to do their loading for them.

Only the Sludge had been made to work. Granny Fang had made her.

'Someone's gotta see she works an' you're the one she's most scared of—so go on and stop your moaning or I'll brand your bum with the poker.' That's what Granny had said. She'd said it with a lovely smile to show off her sharp, filed teeth and make the Sludge more respectful. Granny always kept a poker red hot in the school boiler in case the Sludge got uppish.

'That's another thousand quid you owe me, Batty,'

croaked a husky voice. This was the first bit of conversation that little Caroline Crisp heard. She recognised
that husky croak; it was Mrs Fang. She was playing
cards with the other dinner ladies.

'When are you going to pay me, my girl?' continued
Granny. 'You never paid me last week—nor the week
before!'

'How can I pay you if I ain't got no money?' cackled
little Batty merrily.

'Just you wait,' croaked Granny gleefully, 'you'll
have plenty of it soon!'

'When?' asked Batty eagerly.

'Yes—when?' cried the Sludge who had trudged up
to where Granny and Batty were playing cards with
Mrs Slow, the other dinner lady—the one that was far
thicker than average.

'We've been in this rotten school for weeks,' complained the Sludge in her harsh, grumbling voice. 'I'm
sick of this dinner lady lark. When are we going to do a
job?'

'Yeh,' agreed another voice—a slow, dim, durbrained sort of voice. 'You said you had a job lined up
for us!'

'You gotta job!' shrieked Batty in her merry, mad,
batty, gurgling cackle. 'You gotta job all right—dinner
lady—that's a job, init?'

'Dinner lady!' groaned Sludge. 'I'm fed up with
being a dinner lady. It's worse than jail it is. You don't
'ave no kids cheeking you in jail. I'd rather be there

any day!'

'Would you?' hissed Granny Fang. It was a menacing hiss; Caroline felt frightened but not enough to stop peering. Granny's grim hiss continued: 'Sit down, Sludge, and shut up!'

Sludge sat down.

'Now keep your mouths shut and your ears open!' snapped Granny. 'All of you!'

'I'm not stopping 'ere; not with them blooming kids!' muttered the Sludge.

'No. No more am I,' said the slow, dim, dur voice of Slow.

'Your mouth's too big for your brain—that's your trouble,' snapped Granny Fang. She might have been talking to Sludge or Slow—Caroline couldn't tell.

'That's right,' gurgled little Batty. 'Let Granny do the thinking. She's the boss!'

'Time we 'ad a new one!' That was a whisper—a very low whisper that Sludge made to Slow. But low as it was, and old as she was, Granny heard it.

'Batty,' she said firmly, 'get me the poker!'

After that there was a lot of running about and gasping. Eventually from somewhere out of sight, the Sludge moaned, 'Don't, Granny!'

'Well shut up and don't give me no more lip!'

'All right.'

'Now,' said Granny Fang as she settled herself back in her chair, 'what was the last job we pulled?'

'The orphanage, weren't it?' said Mrs Slow slowly.

'Didn't we break into the orphanage and nick all the toys?'

'That was ages ago,' sighed Granny.

'Yeh!' sniggered Mrs Slow. 'Fink of all them little orphans waking up and finding their toys gone!'

'Serves 'em right,' growled Sludge, 'for being kids. I hate kids! Nasty, noisy, messy, smelly, little things! Always runnin' round crashin' into each other! I hate 'em!'

'Yeh!'

'I hates feeding 'em!'

'Yeh!'

'Shut up about kids!' sighed Granny wearily. 'And answer my question, Sludge! What was the last job we done?'

'The police raffle!'

'Exactly,' agreed Granny Fang grinning like a friendly shark. 'We nicked the police raffle money, didn't we?'

'Yeh!'

'We sneaked right into the police station while they was all watching "Come Dancing" and nicked it from under their big noses!'

'Yeh! Yeh! That's what we did!' agreed Slow.

'And then you, Slow, you went and took a helmet, didn't you?'

'Yeh! I've always wanted one—to keep under my bed for a potty— nice and comfy . . . .'

'So you just picked up a helmet, didn't you, as we

was all sneaking out?'

'Yeh!'

'And then what happened?'

'They chased us.'

'Yes. And why did they chase us? Because the helmet what you went and grabbed was on one of their heads, wasn't it?'

'Yeh!'

'Blimey, Slow, you ain't half half-witted,' grumbled Sludge.

'So they all saw us, didn't they?' continued Granny. 'And those of 'em what could tear themselves away from "Come Dancing" went and chased off after us, didn't they?'

'Yeh, but they couldn't catch us!'

'No—but they all saw us, didn't they? They knows what we looks like now. They knows we look ugly....'

'Yeh!'

'...and savage....'

'Yeh!'

'...and that you looks thick and evil....'

'Yeh!'

'...and Batty looks like she was escaped out of the funny farm....'

'Yeh!'

'...and Sludge looks like a wart-hog....'

'Yeh!'

'So they've all been out lookin' for us, haven't they? 'Cos there's nuffink what gets further up a copper's nose than 'avin' somethink nicked from right under it. See?'

'Yeh!'

'They hates it! All the other coppers laugh at 'em and call 'em names!'

'Yeh!'

'So they've been out looking for us and that's why we came 'ere!'

'What do you mean?' Slow could not quite follow Granny's line of thought.

'It's obvious, init?' cried little Batty butting in merrily. 'Where's the best place for rough, tough, ugly, evil ladies to hide where no one will notice 'em? A school of course! 'Cos no one will see anything out of the ordinary!'

'What do you think we've been doing 'ere for a month slaving over them brats?' cried Granny. 'Being dinner ladies we just blend in—see?'

'Yeh!'

'But the heat's off now,' explained Granny patiently. 'I've just heard that some clever young villain has gone and nicked all their silver cups what they've won for ballroom dancing, and so the cops have forgotten all about their raffle. So we can chuck the dinner lady lark and go out thieving as usual.'

'Yeh! Yeh! Yeh!'

'You mean we don't have to do no washing up?' asked the Sludge.

''Course not!'

'Good!' grinned the happy Sludge. She grabbed a great pile of custard-crusted bowls and hurled them through the air at Batty.

''Ere you are, Batty!' she shrieked. 'Catch!'

But Batty wasn't paying attention. She was looking out through the serving hatch; something had caught her eye. Something that looked like a swarm of freckles.

CRASH!

3

CRASH

In case you are wondering why that crash has a box round it, the reason is that it is supposed to be a muffled crash. This is because that is what Wayne Drain, Craig Vague and everyone else in the school heard when the pile of plates landed on the floor. No one paid any attention; there were often muffled crashes coming from the kitchens. After the muffled crash there were some muffled screams like this:

EEEK!

and

Ahhh!

Also some muffled shouting that sounded like this:

Oka—Oka!

That was Slow yelling, 'Poke her with your poker!'

No one in the classroom paid these faraway crashes and cries any attention. Certainly not Craig and Wayne; they had problems of their own: BIG PROBLEMS.

Miss Thrasher was taking their class that afternoon because their own teacher had had to go and see the doctor about something too horrible to mention. So we won't mention it. Unless, of course, you would particularly like to know. Would you? I see.

Well, it was boils where it was especially difficult to sit down. He was called Herbert Lennon, but the children called him Sherbet Lemon because he was so sweet. People like Wayne Drain kept saying things like, 'Why don't you sit down, sir, and have a nice rest.' But he hardly ever did—only when he forgot—then he'd leap up again as if he'd sat on something hot. Now you know.

Well, while Sherbet Lemon was having his boils admired down at the doctor's, Miss Thrasher took the third year juniors. They were just sitting there looking bored when: Vroom. Vroom. Vroom. Motorbikes! In the playground!

Four enormous bikes zoomed through the play-ground past the classroom window and shot out of the school gates. The dinner ladies were all in studded leather jackets and helmets with horns, so it was difficult to tell which was which. There was a mysterious girl-sized bundle tied onto the back of one machine. It looked suspiciously as if one of the vast curtains in the dining room had been ripped down to wrap something up with.

'We can go to the kitchen now to see if Caroline's okay,' whispered Wayne to Craig.

'Yes,' Craig blinked dreamily.

Miss Thrasher had not noticed that Caroline wasn't there because she wasn't their usual teacher; all the boys needed to do was ask to go to the toilet and then sneak to the kitchen instead.

'Miss, Miss, please—please can I go to the ....'

'You should have gone at dinner time, Wayne. Sit down and shut up!'

'Yes, Miss.'

'Now, can I have a volunteer to help me?' Craig Vague put up his hand dreamily. Miss Thrasher smiled at him; she looked like Dracula smiling at a blood donor.

'Please, Miss, can I go to the ....'

'Yes, Craig, of course you can help. How pleasant it is to see someone in this wretched class who is keen. Now just step out here and press this button every time I do this—'

Miss Thrasher went click with a special clicker she had in her hand. It was a little bit of metal, that was all,

and whenever she bent it there was a loud click.

Craig was worried; the button was on the end of a bit of flex that went into a slide projector. He didn't like slide projectors and things like that; vague people are far too absentminded to deal with machines.

'Now pull the curtains, children,' Miss Thrasher ordered brightly. She was in quite a good mood. 'We're going to see some slides of my holiday looking for ancient flint arrowheads in the great Dartmoor bog!'

A low groan greeted this remark, followed by ripping, tearing sounds as a team of curtain pullers went to work. Then the door opened, and Mrs Pile, the school secretary popped in and murmured into Miss Thrasher's ear.

'Children, just sit quietly. I have to talk to someone important on the telephone,' she told them. 'I will not be long and if, on my return, I see the *smallest sign* of mischief—you will *all* be thrashed!'

As soon as the Thrasher had gone, a great number of interesting things happened:

1 The lights went out.
2 Lottie Blot's plaits got tied together—hard.
3 Wayne Drain got kicked in the pants by Fatty Hardcastle.
4 Fatty Hardcastle got smacked round the earhole by Wayne Drain.
5 Tiny Tina Toot screamed because something cold and slimy had been dropped down the back of her

neck. I think it was one of Fatima Zonk's pet slugs.

6 Craig Vague decided it was now time to go down to the kitchen to see if Caroline was okay.

7 There was a crash.

Yes, Craig had forgotten he was still holding the button on the end of the flex, so long before he got to the door—*Crash*—the slide projector and its special wheel-like thing that all the slides were packed into clattered to the floor.

A sick feeling hit Craig in the tummy. His knees went wobbly. What had he done?

Click. That was Fatty Hardcastle turning the lights back on.

'Cor!'

'Craig!'

'Now you've done it!'

'You'll be for it!'

Craig's mouth went dry. 'Maybe it's not broken,' he said huskily.

'Quick!' said Wayne, stepping up to the wreckage. 'Put it all back before she comes. She'll just think a fuse has gone or something. Come on! Put all those slides back in quick!'

'Okay.'

Children came clustering round to help; slides were picked off the floor and stuffed hastily back into the wheel-like thing.

'Here she comes!' cried Fatty, who had been

on watch.

The door swung open, and Miss Thrasher bounded briskly into the classroom hoping to catch someone being naughty. But all was quiet and peaceful. Yes, the keen, hard-working third years were eagerly reading their maths books. Only Craig Vague was out of his place; he was standing innocently where she had left him, holding the button and waiting patiently.

'Good,' thought the Thrasher to herself. 'It only goes to show that if you threaten children with a good thrashing, they behave themselves!'

She smiled her Dracula smile and switched on the slide projector. Everyone took a deep breath—especially Craig.

It worked! A great beam of light shot out onto the white screen.

'Lights!' ordered Miss Thrasher calmly. The lights went out. 'Now, Craig, remember to press the button when I *click*—I'm going to be near the screen so I can point out the most interesting features of the flints.' She walked briskly to the screen and started her lecture: 'This expedition took place last summer and the first picture shows my friend Professor Watford Smith and myself . . . .'

Click.

' . . . examining our maps—Craig, I went *click*, wake up! As I said, here are Professor Watford Smith and myself . . . .'

Click.

Two dog-faced baboons suddenly appeared fighting over a banana.

There was a roar of laughter from the third-year class! Silly things like that seem to make the modern brat hoot and bray and splutter and honk. They went on doing it for ages!

But there was one member of that class who was not laughing. Not at all. Being wrapped up in a canteen curtain was nothing to laugh about. Being gagged and tied up with tight cords that bit into you—that was no fun either. But the really *frightening* thing was being lashed onto the back of Batty's motorbike as she hurtled along shrieking and gurgling and swerving at people to give them a fright. Batty loved to give people frights and the person she was frightening most was Caroline Crisp.

There was a hole in the curtain that Caroline could see through if she wanted, but most of the time she was so terrified she kept her eyes closed tight. 'We're going to crash! We're going to crash!' she kept thinking fearfully to herself. Then she'd open her eyes for a peep and she'd see something awful—like a bus coming straight at them, or a brick wall—so she'd shut her eyes tight again and scream into her gag.

The trouble was, the dinner ladies didn't seem to bother about which side of the road they were driving down. Granny Fang rode directly down the middle— right down the white line—and the rest of her gang rode behind her in a V formation.

Slow was okay; she was the one on Granny's left; Sludge was next to her riding on the pavement, but Batty was out on the right—racing into all the oncoming traffic. What made it even worse was that Batty kept doing death-defying tricks to show everyone what a dare-devil she was. Years before she'd been a motorcycle girl in a stunt show. In those days she was called *the lovely Trixy* and she'd worn a glamorous Super Woman style costume and done death-defying stunts like wall-of-death riding where you zoom round and round halfway up a wall, while everyone gasps and goes: *'Cor!'*

Batty had not stayed very long in that job because she hated routine. Even so, she was at it long enough to become extra brilliant at riding motorbikes; and, after four weeks cooped-up being a dinner lady, she was in a very frisky mood. Yes, she was in a mood for risks!

Sometimes Batty would zoom off down a side street or through a supermarket but she always found the others again so she must have known where they were going. She gave a great whoop of joy when they got to Marks and Spencer's and shot inside scattering shoppers right and left. She actually stopped in the booze section and cheerfully helped herself to a bottle.

'What are you doing?' roared an important man in a suit.

'I'm doing my shopping,' squawked Batty. 'What does it look like?' Then she started swigging and slurping.

'But you can't ride a motorbike in here! You can't just park it in the middle of . . . .'

'Oh yes I can!' cried Batty. ''Cos I'm disabled!' Then she began to limp back to her bike while the manager gaped.

It was frustrating for Caroline, stopping in the

middle of a shop like that. She couldn't shout, 'Help!'
because of her gag but she *moved* as much as she could
and sort of *growled* as loud as possible. It did no good,
though, because the manager and everyone else were
staring at Batty with rapt attention. It's not every day a
mad bat in a horned helmet rides a motorbike round
Marks and Spencer's, and when it happens people are

apt to forget their manners and stare.

'Catch!' yelled Batty throwing the half-empty bottle at the manager's head; then she leapt onto her bike again and roared off. She seemed to know a special short cut through Marks and Spencer's—out of the back—into Woolworth's—out of the back—into Debenham's—up all the escalators—and onto the roof garden. She rode three times round the roof garden restaurant going faster and faster each time.

Crash! That was a table getting upset

Eeek! That was a waitress getting upset.

Ahhh!

That muffled Ahhh! was Caroline: she was a bit upset too. But Batty was not upset. No, she was gurgling with glee. 'Now for the death-defying leap trick!' she screamed.

As you know, you're supposed to do the death-defying leap trick over fifteen parked cars; only there didn't seem to be any parked cars on the roof garden. So she just took off over the edge— *Bonk* — and landed on top of a multi-storey car park on the other side of the street.

Caroline had opened her eyes when she'd heard the waitress go *Eeek!* so she'd seen the death-defying leap trick as well as felt that sickening, sinking, big-dipper

31

feeling that you get when you're hurtling through the air. On the whole, Caroline would rather have been at home watching 'Blue Peter'.

4

Miss Thrasher wasn't as savage as all that. I mean she didn't run around biting people when the third year juniors hooted and chortled at the two baboons. She just stopped them laughing by saying in an extra icy voice, 'Most amusing!' Then she looked sharply at Craig before deciding that he was just *too* dreamy to have pulled off such a smart trick by himself.

'Very well,' she told the third years, 'since you appear to have *no interest whatsoever* in the very import-ant bits of flint that Professor Watford Smith and I found in the bog—I will not *bore* you by showing you the slides! And I will *cancel* the trip I was intending to take you on to see the flints in Professor Watford Smith's famous collection at the Wildlife Park . . . .'

At the words 'Wildlife Park' a sudden change of mood swept over the third year juniors. Instead of looking a bit bored, mixed up with a bit of sniggery, they all suddenly looked amazed and deeply hurt.

'Yes!' cried the Thrasher in a serves-you-right voice. 'Those baboons which you found *so* amusing are part of Professor Watford Smith's Wildlife Park which you *would have* been able to see had you *behaved* yourselves!'

Anxious cries of, 'Oh, Miss! Please, Miss! We didn't mean to, Miss!' were heard. Then Wayne started off on a good tack: raising his hand in an eager, keen way, he politely asked if Professor Watford Smith was an explorer.

'Indeed he is!' answered Miss Thrasher. The serves-you-right tone was on the way down by now, and her how-nice-to-see-you-are-so interested tone was on the way up. 'Watford Smith is the most famous archaeologist and explorer in England. He has discovered a fortune in treasure; he has a wonderful collection of wild animals; he dug up the famous bogwitch....'

Cries of 'Cor!' and Phew!' and 'Brill!' could be heard. Those cunning little third year juniors knew how to suck up to teachers really brilliantly. Wayne Drain stuck up his hand again and politely and keenly asked about the bogwitch. Apparently it was a witch that had been dug out of a bog. Okay?

'Is it alive, Miss?'

'No, Tina, of course not.'

Then Lottie Blot put up her hand and gazed at Miss Thrasher with her special, extra-simpering gaze and spoke with her special deeply-respectful, creeping voice: 'Is Professor Watford Smith very handsome, Miss?' she asked. Nobody sniggered. Everyone waited.

'Well,' replied the Thrasher, 'he has—er—a certain manly charm. A—er—rugged look.'

'Is he very tall, Miss?'

'Tall? Yes—tall—for someone who is, er, small.'

'Does he have adventures, Miss? I mean is he very brave?'

'Well, he—er—certainly leads a very exciting

34

life, Lottie.'

Craig was still standing out in front of the class because it had not occurred to him to return to his place. He tried to picture what this Watford Smith looked like; a nervous dwarf with a red nose. That's what he imagined. He stood in front of the class trying not to smile at this mental picture. But he did not succeed. A grin appeared on his dreamy face.

This was exactly the wrong time for the rest of them to see a grin. Everyone was sucking up really expertly. Then they saw Craig's grin and Belinda Bat honked out the words: 'Is he your boyfriend, Miss?'

Hoots. Smirks. Chortles. Sniggers. Those unfortunate third years just couldn't stop laughing.

'Certainly not. Now, as we are *not* going to see the Wildlife Park, the bogwitch, the treasure, or anything else of the professor's, I suggest we change the subject. Get out your maths books. *Now!*'

Craig Vague was worried. What was the meaning of that tattoo, he wondered. And had Caroline really just gone home by herself after the dinner ladies had roared off? Why hadn't she come back to the classroom? Scared of the dreaded Thrasher perhaps? Scared of being thrashed for being late?

Maybe. Maybe the dinner ladies had kidnapped her!

When you are walking along thinking hard, you tend to walk further then you intended. That's what happened to Craig. His mum was just wondering where he was and had looked out of the front window when she saw this boy wandering past the house deep in thought.

She was just quietly muttering to herself and sighing and generally relaxing so she would be on top form when her little son finally appeared, when there was a ring at the door. It was Wayne.

'Can Craig come out?' he asked.

There was a sigh. Then she said, 'No. I'm afraid he can't, Wayne, because he hasn't got back from school yet.'

'What?' Wayne was amazed.

'You see, Wayne, it takes Craig rather longer than most people to do the most simple things. You should know that.'

'Yes,' agreed Wayne politely. Then, feeling that perhaps he ought to say something to help his dreamy friend, he remarked, 'He's got a lot on his mind.'

'A lot of what on his mind?' asked Craig's mother in a long-suffering sort of voice. 'Sawdust?'

Wayne laughed respectfully.

'Well,' she said, 'you'd better come in and wait for him if you want to see him.'

This was lucky for Craig because it meant that instead of having a five-star fit when he arrived, his mum merely raised her eyebrows so that they practically disappeared and shook her head in a slow, sad way. 'Where's your bag?' was all she said.

Wayne sniggered and Craig's mum glided away

looking hard pressed and long suffering. As soon as the door closed Craig said, 'I thwonkswijow!' This means, 'I think Caroline's been kidnapped by the dinner ladies!' That's how it comes out when you say it with your mouth full of bread and jam.

Wayne chortled when he understood. He didn't really believe it and, for that matter, neither did Craig.

But pretending is good fun and pretending not to be pretending makes it better.

'We'll be detectives!' cried Wayne.

'Yeh!'

'*Ace* detectives! I'll be the chief one who always solves the crimes, and you can be the thick one who always has to have everything explained to him, okay?'

'No. You should be the thick one 'cos it would be easier for you—more natural!'

'Oh yeh!'

'Yeh!'

And so it was they started the Ace Detective team of *Drain and Vague* or *Vague and Drain* (depending on which one was telling you about it).

'You be back before seven!' yelled Mrs Vague as the fearless crimebusters left the house. 'And don't go down by the ....'

Slam!

There's a pub down by the canal which is called 'The Artful Snatcher'. It's a place to steer clear of unless you are a mugger, or a burglar, or a gangster, or an artful snatcher. Are you one of these? Well, steer clear of it or you'll be in trouble. Big trouble. That's where Caroline Crisp had been taken and she was in trouble. Big trouble!

5

Whenever a skinhead banged his head against another skinhead's head, there was this horrible, hollow clunk. They were head-banging you see, the special skinhead way. There was a rock group playing in the corner of the main bar of the 'The Artful Snatcher' and all the muggers and snatchers were dancing with their wild girlfriends. I expect you have heard of heavy metal groups; well, this one was a scrap metal group, which is almost the same except that whenever a scrap breaks out they stop playing and join in, whereas a heavy metal group just carries on so that people can hit each other in time to the music.

A roar of revving motorbikes outside drowned the scrap metal music for a few seconds. Then the motorbikes stopped; the doors flew open and the dinner ladies appeared. They stayed at the threshold for a minute or two because Sludge and Slow both tried to barge in at once and, being built like haystacks, got stuck until Granny barged them from behind. Last of all, in came merry little Batty dragging something behind her wrapped up in an old curtain.

Clunk. Bonk. Bong. Bump went this mysterious parcel as she dragged it upstairs to the private room that gangs used when they wanted to plan jobs in peace.

'What you got there, Batty?' asked Granny Fang

lighting up her pipe and settling comfily in an easy chair.

Batty heaved her bundle up onto the table and undid it. The other dinner ladies were not pleased to see Caroline.

'What you bring 'er 'ere for?' snapped the Sludge.

'I told you to get rid of 'er!' growled Granny.

'You said you was gonna mince her in the mincer!' said the slow, dur voice of Slow.

'Well, I changed my mind,' cried Batty defiantly. 'I'm going to keep her; I'm gonna train her up to be a thief! I'm getting old. We're all getting old—and *some of us* are getting fat. We need a keen young thief to do the clambering and climbing and the slithering and all that.'

'I says you should've minced her!' That was still Granny's opinion.

'Yeh! Minced her!' agreed the others.

Batty had been good at working the mincing machine; she'd minced all sort of nutritious things for those lucky children—fresh worms, for example, and mice—plenty of mice because the kitchen had been plagued by them.

'Mice and rice was nice,' she gurgled. 'Them kids used to love it! They was always asking for seconds.'

'They wouldn't have if they'd known what the rice was!' laughed Sludge. The rice hadn't really been rice, you see, but boiled maggots which look (and taste) just the same but are much cheaper.

'Shut up about mincing mice. It's *her* what you ought to have minced!' growled Granny. She glared at Caroline who was sitting on the table crying. Tears were oozing out of her green eyes, tumbling down her freckled cheeks, and seeping into her gag.

'She'll be okay,' claimed Batty. 'She reminds me of myself when I was her age. When I first saw 'er I remembered the time when I was just a little vandal runnin' round smashin' things up and writing rude words on walls. Which would you prefer, my sweetheart—being an apprentice thief or being put through the mincer? Which would you like, my lovely? Just nod your 'ead if you wants to be a thief. See, girls! What did I say! She's nodding 'er sweet, little head!'

The other three were unimpressed. They glared at Caroline and muttered. Then Batty gave one of her shrieks and clapped her hands excitedly. 'Here!' she squawked. 'We could work the old three-armed-nun dodge!'

'Yeh!'

'Yeh!'

'Yeh!'

After this inspired thought, the dinner ladies seemed much happier about having Caroline as an apprentice. They kept her tied up, though, just in case she went wandering off and got lost. But they did send Slow down for some Coke and a packet of crisps for her.

'I 'spect you likes crisps seeing as how you're called

42

Crisp,' cackled Batty undoing Caroline's gag.

'I'm not very hungry,' sobbed the apprentice.

''Course you are!' gurgled Batty. 'You eat up. You needs all your strength you do when you're out thieving.'

'When am I going to start?' asked Caroline tearfully.

'Right now!' cried Granny. 'No time like the present!'

'Good grief!' cried a superior voice. A boy's voice. It came from the bridge over the canal.

'What?' cried another.

'I do declare! A pair of dim, dur-brained bone-heads from Littlesprat Primary School!'

'What!' cried the second boy. 'Not *the* Littlesprat School where the children are so *thick*?'

'Yes—that's the place. Look at them down there by the canal trying to catch fish with a coathanger! It's pathetic!'

'WE ARE NOT TRYING TO CATCH FISH!' roared Wayne at the two watching Wallies. They were Wallies, you see, from St. Wally's School.

'I think one of them spoke,' said the first Wally.

'Yes. It seems to be able to talk!' said the other.

'WE'RE DRAGGING THE CANAL!' yelled Wayne.

'Fancy! They're *dragging* the canal! *Where* are you dragging it?' The oh-so-clever Wallies sniggered and spluttered merrily.

'We're dragging it for clues!'

'Clues?'

'Yes. We're detectives!'

A lot of honking and spluttering greeted this explanation.

'But my *dear* dim Littlesprats, don't you know you have to have *brains* to be detectives?'

The Ace Detectives ignored this wounding remark and carried on with their important task. They were going to drag a hook through the canal to see if any vital clues were in there. This is the sort of thing detectives did, you see. But it was really difficult dragging a canal with one of Mrs Vague's coathangers—just the thing for hanging coats on, but for dragging canals they were useless.

Splash! That was Craig throwing in the coathanger on the end of a length of string.

'It's floating!' shrieked a Wally gleefully.

'Must be 'cos it's made of plastic!' gurgled the other.

Then the Wallies amused themselves by jumping up and down like apes and scratching themselves, ape-like, under their arms, and going *'Dur!'* It was *humiliating*.

So the Ace Detectives never managed to drag the canal. They just stood there being jeered at and trying to think of something smart to say or something tough to do. Then the Wallies disappeared and they were by themselves again.

Wayne hurled a stone into the icy waters. 'There's all

sorts of clues in there,' he sighed as he watched the ripples reflecting the street lights. 'Some other detectives with the right sort of hooks will come and discover them!'

'Yeh,' agreed Craig. 'Like Wallies! They might have the right stuff!'

'Yeh! They might come and drag the canal and get all the clues and rescue Caroline,' grumbled Wayne.

'Then they'd get the reward!'

The boys were pretending that Caroline's dad had offered a huge reward for finding her.

'Actually,' sighed Wayne, 'if I was Caroline's dad, I'd offer a huge reward to keep her kidnapped!'

That was a good one; Craig laughed.

'The fact is,' Wayne continued, 'nothing bad ever really happens round here. It's the wrong area to be detectives in. Everything is so boring.'

'Yeh.'

Craig looked at the canal. It was a *boring* canal. He looked up at the bridge; it was a *boring* bridge. They heard footsteps and clambered up the path to the street. But they were *boring* footsteps—just some funny old nuns plodding peacefully past.

'There's nothing going on round here,' sighed Craig.

The bored detectives mooched down Newlands Road and through the little lane that leads into Townsend Avenue. They found a suspicious cat sitting on a wall there and kept it under surveillance for three minutes.

'We've got our eyes on you, Cat!' Wayne warned. 'So don't try anything funny!' The cat yawned.

They crept softly and sneakily into Douglas Crescent so as to look in through people's lighted windows for clues.

'That looks suspicious!' whispered Craig, pointing at a suspicious tree.

'That looks really suspicious!' hissed Wayne pointing at a suspicious car that was parked suspiciously next to the pavement. 'A *new* car. You know what that means?'

'Yeh. It means it's not an old one!'

'Exactly! Shine your torch at it. Give it a fright!'

'Okay.'

Craig had this torch which didn't need batteries. It had a trigger beside the handle and you had to keep squeezing and releasing this trigger to make it shine. The faster you did it, the more light you got. Squeezing hard made your hand ache, so Craig didn't do it very vigorously. Dribbles of light oozed out of the torch and dimly lit up the inside of the car. There was nothing much inside—just a pink exercise book on the back seat with childish writing on the cover: *Caroline Crisp— Social Studies.*

Suddenly the Ace Detectives became serious. Craig squeezed furiously at his torch until a beam like a searchlight lit up this startling clue.

'That's Caroline's Social Studies book!' he said after careful thought.

'Stop the torch!' whispered Wayne. 'They might see us!'

'Okay.'

'What shall we do?'

'Dunno!'

'I know!'

'What?'

'Let the tyres down, of course! So they can't make a getaway! Then, soon as we've let the tyres down, we can get the police!'

'Right,' hissed Craig, 'how do you let tyres down?'

'Same as on a bike, I expect. Squeeze your torch again—softly.'

'Okay.'

Wayne was right about letting down car tyres. First you unscrew the dust-cap, just like on a bike, then you press the top of the valve with a penknife.

Air was hissing out of the tyre nicely when a cold hand gripped Wayne fiercely by the ear.

6

'What do you think you're doing?'

'Nothing, Miss.'

'What do you mean, "nothing", you wretched boy! You're letting the air out of my tyres!' Miss Thrasher's grip on the ear did *not* relax.

'We didn't know it was your car,' explained Craig.

'You mean to tell me your idea of fun is to go around letting the air out of car tyres at random?'

'No, Miss, but . . . .'

'This is a most serious matter!'

The Thrasher was highly steamed up. 'Behaviour of this sort goes far beyond the usual boyish pranks!' she told Wayne's dad on the 'phone. Wayne's dad agreed.

Then Miss Thrasher 'phoned Craig's house. Mrs Vague went pale when she heard what a fiend her son was.

'And that is why I wish to punish them *right now*,' the Thrasher told her.

'You're not going to thrash them, are you?' asked Craig's mum anxiously.

'No. With your permission, I will use them to help me with some heavy work; I already have them pumping up my tyre and I could do with some help carrying boxes of flint.'

Craig's mum thought that was fair. If the boys had

been caught letting down Miss Thrasher's tyres, then it was reasonable that they should be made to help her carry her boxes. It would serve them right and they would learn their lesson. That's what she thought and Wayne's dad had thought the same.

'Be careful! Don't drop anything! Don't just dump them! Put them down gently! Mind the paint work! That's a new car!' That was some of the friendly advice that the Thrasher gave them as they loaded up her car with heavy wooden boxes stuffed with flints. They had to go backwards and forwards from her house to the car, and every journey made them more zapped.

'Now where do you think you're going?' asked the Thrasher when they'd finished.

'Home.'

'Oh no you're not! You're coming with me to *unload* them again at the other end!'

'At the other end of what?' asked Craig.

'At the other end of my journey!' she snapped.

It was a bit scary being driven by the Thrasher. The two boys sat on the back seat next to Caroline's Social Studies book listening to her grumbling about all the marking she had to do. They both knew she had this special marking machine which stamped books with red crosses but they didn't say anything. They didn't even ask where they were going; suddenly the houses stopped and the fields started. Then the headlights lit up a huge sign:

WATFORD SMITH'S
MUSEUM
AND WILDLIFE PARK

it said in big letters, then, in small ones it continued:

VISIT THE BOGWITCH

SEE OUR FAMOUS WART-HOGS

SEE MONKEY ISLAND

WATCH THE LIONS FEED

Wayne and Craig perked up.

'Don't get any ideas about having fun!' growled Miss Thrasher. 'You're here to work; and I'm here to see you do!'

They were driving down a long drive with high fencing on either side. No doubt the lions and other animals were behind the fences, but the boys couldn't see anything. The car stopped in front of a grand mansion with all its downstairs windows lit. Other cars were arriving and people were swarming up the steps; a beard was standing on the top step.

Yes. An enormous, black beard with a pair of glasses in it was standing by the door greeting everyone. He grabbed people's hands and shook them so vigorously the glasses started to slide. Then he pushed them back into place and beamed through them cheerily. This enormous beard (together with the glasses) leapt down the steps when it saw the Thrasher.

'Prudence!' it gurgled gleefully. 'How lovely to see

you! Have you brought the flints? Ah! And who are these fine young chaps?'

'They are delinquents!' Miss Thrasher told him gravely. 'On *no* account are you to be nice to them, Watford. They are here to hump boxes about; they are not here to enjoy themselves!'

'Good heavens! Why not?'

'Because,' replied the Thrasher, 'their idea of enjoying themselves is creeping about the streets letting people's tyres down!'

There was a gurgle from the bearded one, followed by an eerie snorting; the glasses nearly fell out of the beard and a hairy hand emerged to prod them back into place.

The place those glasses were supposed to occupy was the space immediately in front of Professor Watford Smith's little brown eyes but, unfortunately, his nose was so small that they tended to shoot off it. Normally he stuck them to his ears with sticky tape but tonight he was being especially posh because of all the people coming to his museum. Watford Smith looked like a huge furry ball with glasses. He bounced a lot too—just like an extra-bouncy, fur-lined ball. Of course he was wearing clothes, but, as these seemed to be the same colour as his beard, they blended in.

'No, no, no, no, no—NO!' he cried when Prudence Thrasher started to stand over the boys and tell them what to do. 'No, no, no, NO!' he laughed. 'The delinquents and I will manage the boxes— you go on in and—er—mingle. Seize a sausage! Have a drink!'

'Really, Watford, I must . . . .'

'No, no, no, no, no! In you GO!'

She began to climb the steps.

'Yes, yes, yes, yes—keep going!'

So she did.

'Now,' beamed the beard adjusting his specs once again. 'Let's have these boxes out.' He swooped onto a box and tucked it under his arm, then balanced another on top of it. Finally he tottered up the steps carrying all the boxes and yelling at the boys, 'Follow me! Let's get some grub for you—it's hungry work lugging boxes about!'

'Doesn't the park shut at night?' asked Wayne as he darted up the steps behind the great explorer.

'Yes, yes. Of course. We don't want hordes of people milling about all the time. The Wildlife Park closes at five. So does the museum.'

'But who are all these people?'

'People?' answered the puzzled prof. 'People? These people aren't *people*—they are history teachers.'

'Cor!'

'Yes, dear boy, all the history teachers for miles around are here tonight. It's the autumn meeting of the Cobweb Club, the special club for history teachers.'

They were inside the great house by now and the boys could see all the history teachers yapping at each other. It was not a pretty sight; half of them looked as if they spent all their time digging things up, and the

53

other half looked as if they'd been dug up by the first lot.

'What?' cried Wayne. 'Are all these people history teachers?'

'Yes, yes, yes.'

'What—like those nuns?'

Professor Watford Smith glanced in the direction Wayne was pointing; four beefy looking nuns were standing in a huddle nattering.

'I suppose so,' answered the Professor pushing his glasses back onto his nose again. 'Nuns can be teachers, you know.'

'What about Miss Thrasher?'

'Well,' he replied, 'she's just popped over with the flints we found on Dartmoor. I'm going to show them to the history teachers. History teachers like that sort of thing, you know.'

'Yes.'

So Miss Thrasher will be taking you back home shortly. Never mind, dear boys, you may have to miss the learned meeting of the Cobweb Club, but I'm sure they can spare you a cold sausage or two. Help yourselves.'

It's worrying when sausages disappear. If you are just happily chomping a sausage and thinking to yourself, 'This is a frightfully good sausage—I'm glad I've another one exactly the same on my funny little cardboard plate,' then it's worrying when you look eagerly at the remaining sausage and find it's not there

any more.

The scientists of the world have examined the facts and are all agreed: sausages can't fly. So what happened to it? That's what Miss Thrasher wondered when her last sausage vanished. She looked grimly about the crowded room for sausage snatchers; someone must have snitched it—that was her opinion. One of those wretched boys!

But they were far away in a corner scoffing platefuls of grub of their own and doing their best to avoid her. She looked at the nearest members of the Cobweb Club; there were only a couple of nuns near her, neither of whom had a sausage stick in her hand. Besides, nuns don't go around stealing sausages.

'I must be losing my grip,' thought the Thrasher sadly. 'Years of dealing with brats has driven me to the brink of madness; I must have *imagined* I had another sausage.'

Teachers often go mad, as I expect you realise. There is a special loony-bin for them called the Dunyellin Rest Home, where no children or chalk or red ink or horrible dinners are allowed. Everything at Dunyellin is deeply restful but, even so, the Thrasher shuddered when she thought she might be sent there. That's when she saw the ghostly hand. Yes, a hand—all by itself, without an arm or anything—appeared in the air in front of her clutching a half-chewed sausage.

'Gna!' spluttered the Thrasher. (Gna! is what people often splutter when confronted by ghostly hands.) One of the nuns wheeled round to stare at her and then suddenly wheeled back again. Ghostly hands are horrible things to see floating about but when they are small and freckled and holding half-eaten sausages, the horror is *tinged with terror*. You think, 'Gna! How can you eat it without a mouth?'

That's exactly what the Thrasher thought. Then she told herself, 'It *can't* eat because it's not really there! It is a figment of my *mad mind!* I'll pretend I didn't see it. I'll just walk calmly about looking extra sane.' So off she staggered, trying to look normal. It's a good job she was surrounded by history teachers or people might have noticed.

'Look out! She's on the warpath!' muttered Wayne. Craig glanced in the direction Wayne's pained face was pointing; Miss Thrasher was striding along amid the history teachers grinning like a hyena to show everyone how extra-normal she was.

'She looks sort of funny,' remarked Craig, 'sort of even weirder!'

'Yeh.'

'Cor—look. She's not coming this way any more—I thought she was coming to take us home.'

'Yeh, she said she'd only be stopping a minute. She must have forgotten. Great!'

'Yeh—we can scoff some more!'

'Now what's happening?' asked Wayne.

'Dunno.'

The members of the Cobweb Club had stopped

yapping loudly and were now yapping softly. All together it sounded a bit like a hum and a bit like a buzz. They were all moving towards the end of the room where the boys were.

It was eerie, seeing all those history teachers coming towards them buzzing and humming. Craig thought he heard a word being buzzed and hummed a lot. The word was: *Treasure!*

Suddenly the huge, black beard, hairy hands and frisky glasses of Professor Watford Smith pranced and danced up to the two boys.

'As you see, ladies and gentlemen, I have two assistants to help me,' he announced.

Chortle. Honk. Squawk went the Cobweb Club politely.

'Now, I have been asked to show you some of my recent finds. Firstly several boxes of flint arrowheads from the Great Bog of Dartmoor—the same bog in which we found the bogwitch five years ago. I like to think that perhaps the bogwitch might have used some of these flints to clip her toe nails with!'

Honk. Splutter. Chortle. History teachers love weedy jokes like that.

Watford Smith pushed back his spectacles and continued: 'Now my assistants have been busy clearing a space in all this food . . . .'

Honk. Chortle.

' . . . and they will now spread out the flints for you to see. Meanwhile I have in my pocket the really

58

important—not to say glittering—prize I have, er, *unearthed (chortle)* since last we met. I refer, of course, to the priceless Pink Diamond of Portugal which was part of the pirate Blackbeard's treasure. I think, ladies and gentlemen, that you will agree that it is appropriate that I should have been the one that discovered Blackbeard's treasure . . . .'

Chortle. Honk.

' . . . Unfortunately Blackbeard the pirate was somewhat dim. He is assumed to have suffered from what is now known to doctors as, *ear-to-ear bone!'*

Chortle. Squawk.

' . . . Yes. He, er, went about robbing people of the most worthless things. Glass beads, for example, and conkers. His treasure chest was full of marbles and it was not until I had examined them all thoroughly that the pink diamond was identified. Anyway,' beamed Watford Smith, 'here it is . . . .' He fished in his pocket and triumphantly produced—a half-eaten sausage!

7

It's not very nice being an apprentice thief if you think stealing is wrong. Caroline Crisp thought stealing was wrong, even though she sometimes sort of accidentally snitched sweets from her big sister's secret sweety store. But snitching sweets from big sisters isn't really bad because it stops them from rotting their teeth; so in fact it's really a very kind and helpful thing to do.

But being a real thief and having to rob people was really horrible. Caroline kept thinking how vile and evil it was; then she'd think of ways to escape but the dinner ladies kept sharp watch over her.

'You watch 'er, Batty. Don't let 'er out of yer sight or she'll run round the nick and sing 'er little 'ead off.' That's what Granny had said to old Batty while they were still at 'The Artful Snatcher'. Running round the nick and singing means going to the police station and telling, as I expect you realise.

'She aint going to sing!' gurgled Batty. 'Are you, my darling?' Caroline shook her head. ''Cos if you do we'll get you and we'll do for you—won't we, my chick?' Caroline nodded. Everytime she nodded or shook her head it made her tears roll down her cheeks faster.

'You'll soon get used to being a thief,' Batty told her. 'You'll soon learn the art of it. And everytime you do it right you'll 'ave a good meal and all the sweets you can eat. But if you do it wrong you'll get caught and put into jail and you'll have to sew mailbags and eat porridge.'

They had still been up in the special room for planning jobs when Batty said that. Caroline was sitting on the table and the four dinner ladies were sitting round it staring at her.

'Right!' cried Granny grinning so that her shark teeth glinted, 'we're going to do the old three-armed-nun dodge. Slow . . . .'

'Yuh?'.

'Go down stairs and get four nun outfits!'

'Okay.'

Slow shambled off and reappeared a few minutes later dragging a huge box.

'Wot about the snatcher?' growled Sludge with a sharp look at Caroline. 'I'm not 'aving 'er in wiv *me*— I'm not 'aving no little kid worming an' squirming and getting under my feet!'

'No. Not me neither!' spluttered the dur voice of Slow as she struggled into her nun kit.

'Batty can 'ave 'er,' suggested the Sludge, 'seeing as how she lumbered us wiv 'er in the first place.'

There was a frisking of skirts and thrashing of arms as Granny Fang pulled her nun's habit down over herself. 'Batty's not tall enough. It'll have to be you, Sludge. Slow is too thick.'

'No I aint. I aint too thick. I aint thick at all!'

'Then how come you can't get dressed up as a nun

without getting all tangled up?'

'I dunno. It's got stuck. On me 'ead.'

''Course it's stuck on your head. 'Cos you 'aven't took your helmet off, have you? You've got them great horns sticking out of your head like a bison! You great pudding!'

'Why don't you have the snatcher yourself?' asked the Sludge in a challenging tone.

'Do as Granny says, Sludge,' said little Batty. 'She's the boss.'

'Not no longer she ain't!'

'Oh yes,' said Granny quietly, 'and what do you mean by that?'

'I mean your poker's not 'ot no more—that's what I mean!'

'Yeh?'

'Yeh!'

'I don't 'ave to 'ave no hot poker, Sludge, to deal with the likes of you!'

'That's right!' shrieked Batty merrily. 'Granny can use 'er teeth on you any time she wants. She could snap the ears off you!'

Granny grinned her agreement and the Sludge frowned at the sharp, filed, shark teeth.

'She aint the only one what can bite!' growled Sludge opening her mouth to show her own teeth. But Batty's little hand suddenly shot out and snatched Sludge's teeth from out of her gums. They were false, you see.

'Bite!' cried Batty triumphantly. 'You couldn't bite a milk jelly!' She hurled the teeth out of the window with a squawk of joy.

'Right,' said Granny firmly, 'that settles it. The girl goes in with Sludge!'

Now, as you have already worked out with your brilliant brain, the three-armed-nun dodge works like this:

1 You get a huge, gigantic, toothless lady burglar and dress her up as a nun.

2 Then you get a small apprentice thief and put her under the big burglar's nun skirt.

3 There is a special hole in the skirt so that the small thief (or snatcher) can poke a hand out and snatch things. The big 'nun' walks about, looking all respectable and holy with her hands where everyone can see them—but, as she goes past people, the snatcher picks their pockets.

If you want to know what it was like for Caroline being a snatcher, here's what to do:

Find a very large horse.

Walk along behind it so close that your head keeps bumping into its backside.

Drape a most enormous, black blanket over your head so that you are *plunged* into darkness.

That's exactly what it was like being a snatcher with Mrs Sludge, only Mrs Sludge smelt worse.

Clunk! That was Caroline bonking into Sludge.

Stomp! That was Sludge stamping on Caroline's foot.

Gnash! That was Caroline clenching her teeth to stop herself yelling out with pain.

Yow! That was the Sludge yelling out with pain because Caroline bit into her bum when she clenched her teeth.

Ssh! That was Granny Fang.

Luckily no one paid any attention to the big nun going *Yow*; everyone was too busy humming and buzzing about the Pink Diamond of Portugal.

'I had it in my pocket,' cried the professor. 'It was there only a moment ago.' He was so upset he forgot to shove his glasses back and they slid right over his nose. 'It was in a little box,' he explained to the Cobwebbers.

'Little box!' they all hummed and buzzed excitedly. People started looking about for a little box. It could have fallen onto the floor, so they glanced keenly at the carpet.

'Perhaps it's in your beard,' someone suggested helpfully. Watford Smith ran his fingers through his beard; a bit of eggy toast dropped out of it but that was all.

Everyone gazed solemnly at the eggy toast. Then a strange, high-pitched voice was heard: 'You say you found a half-eaten sausage in your pocket instead of the diamond?' It was Miss Thrasher.

'Yes.'

'I saw a—half-eaten sausage a few minutes ago—it was—hovering . . . .'

'Hovering?' cried Professor Watford Smith.

'What—by itself?'

'No. Not by itself. It was—being gripped.'

'What by? What was gripping it?'

'A hand.'

'Whose hand?'

'Just a hand. A human hand—all by itself. I saw it—quite distinctly. In fact I thought I was going mad. But now that the pink diamond has been stolen and a *half-eaten sausage* put in its place, it would seem that I am *not* mad. Not mad at all. In fact it's something far worse!'

'What?' cried the professor.

'A ghost!' cried the Thrasher dramatically. 'I have never really believed in ghosts. But having seen that ghostly hand and having heard about the diamond, that is the only explanation. We have a visitor among us—an *unearthly* one!'

'Yes!' cried one of the teachers. 'I saw a hovering hand as well—a little freckled hand holding a crisp! I—I thought that I was drunk, so said to myself, "Sherbet," I said, "you're seeing things; you should not have had that glass of sherry. You are not used to booze!" That's what I said. So I am very glad to hear that Miss Thrasher has seen the same hovering hand. It proves that I am not as drunk as I thought I was.'

'Perhaps it is the ghost of the bogwitch!' cried another of the history teachers nervously.

After that there was more humming and buzzing; the idea that a ghostly bogwitch was wandering about chewing sausages seemed to worry everybody. Eventually the bearded one held up a hand to stop the humming and buzzing. When it was quiet he said this: 'What Prudence Thrasher has told us about the hovering hand is most disturbing. What we need is a vicar to exorcise it . . . .'

'Exercise it!' gasped the Thrasher. 'I should have thought a P.E. teacher would be better than a vicar!'

'No—a piano teacher,' suggested Sherbet Lemon. 'Since it's only a hand a P.E. teacher would be useless, but a piano teacher could make it do piano exercises.'

The history teachers began to buzz and hum again. They all seemed to agree that it didn't matter what sort of teacher exercised the ghost, just so long as it wasn't a history teacher.

'I said *exorcise* not *exercise!*' cried Watford Smith. 'Exorcism is the casting out of evil spirits; vicars do it for a small fee. Are there any vicars here?'

'No,' answered the Thrasher, 'but there are some nuns. Perhaps they'd do it for a small fee.'

Everyone looked at the nuns. One of them smiled like a shark and said, 'Yeh—we'll do it—for a large fee!' Then the four nuns chuckled softly—a ghastly sound like boiling custard.

'Turn off the lights and keep quiet!' ordered the nun with the filed teeth.

'Now,' she continued when it was dark, 'don't nobody say nothing; I'm going to talk to the evil spirit.' Then her voice went specially important and she called out: 'Is there anybody there?'

'No,' answered a ghostly voice.

'How come you answered if you aint there?'

'Cos you said "any body" and I aint got a body,' explained the ghost eerily.

'Well, what have you got?'

'A hand!'

'Was you the ghostly hand that gripped the sausage?'

'Yes!'

'Was you the little freckled hand what clutched the crisp?'

'Yes!'

'Was it you what stole the diamond?'

'No!'

'Well who did?'

'Them 'orrible little boys!'

Suddenly all the history teachers started buzzing and humming again. It was an angry sound.

8

'Catch them!' yelled the nun with the teeth when the lights came on. She charged the Cobwebbers pushing them aside with her flying elbows.

If Wayne and Craig had been calm, cool and sensible, they'd have stayed where they were and waited while their pockets were searched. There were conkers, bits of string, lots of fluff and some snotty hankies in their pockets, but no pink diamond.

Perhaps you are the sort of person that remains cool and calm at all times. If you were just sitting reading a comic when you heard a thundering sound and looking up, saw four mad nuns charging at you, would you remain cool and calm? Would you coolly and calmly remark, 'Ah, I see I am being charged by four mad nuns,' and then coolly and calmly continue reading your comic? Or would you drop the comic and run? Which? Well Craig and Wayne ran too.

It was a *deeply suspicious* thing to do. Even Professor Watford Smith was deeply suspicious; he remembered what the Thrasher had said about them being delinquents. 'Gosh!' he thought. (People like Watford Smith always say *Gosh* instead of *Cor* or *Cripes* or *Great Globules of Snot!* at moments of crisis.) 'Gosh!' thought the professor seizing his beard and giving it a tug of anguish. 'To think I trusted those little chaps and

69

thought they were honest and true! But were they? No, no, no, no, no, NO! They were false, deceiving thieves!' He tugged his beard again until his little brown eyes were watery.

While the bearded one stood gormlessly gawping, the four strange nuns charged after the fleeing boys. The history teachers watched with wide open eyes, eager to remember everything that happened so that they could write history books about it later. The four ferocious nuns thundered after the boys; after the nuns came Miss Thrasher. Yes, the Thrasher seemed extra-keen to get to grips with Wayne and Craig. She dashed through the gap that the nuns had cut through the history teachers with their flying feet and elbows.

Thwock! Thump! Sock! Eeek! That's what you hear when history teachers get kicked out of the way.

Mutter! Pant! Mutter! Pant! That's what you hear when a Thrasher goes galloping by muttering and panting.

Luckily Wayne and Craig were quick runners; unluckily they were *not* quick thinkers. Quick thinkers would have run *out* of the front door and into the inky night. Quick-thinking types who were also fast runners could have easily escaped by doing that. But Wayne Drain and Craig Vague ran upstairs instead.

'They're still after us!' gasped Wayne looking back down the elegant sweep of the staircase.

'This way!' cried Craig dashing off down a corridor. He thought that dashing down that corridor was the best thing to do because there was a huge sign on the wall with a hand pointing down it. Under the sign were the words: TO THE BOGWITCH.

Neither of the running boys read these words; there wasn't time; all they saw was the pointing finger. So it seemed as if the hand was giving them some friendly advice on the best way of escape.

It was dark upstairs because the lights were off, and neither of the runners was alert enough to stop and switch them on. The further down the corridor they ran, the darker it got. Eventually Craig had to get his special torch out, and feeble dribbles of light oozed out of it. That's how they found the BOGWITCH door.

'In here!' gasped Wayne and barged inside.

A bogwitch is a witch that has been in a bog for thousands of years. People that have been in a bog for that long tend to look a bit eerie, but what made this particular bogwitch especially creepy was that she was lying in an oak chest without a lid. The bogwitch was mummified, gaunt, and grim, with an evil grin fixed in her face like a letterbox.

Craig gripped his torch and a thin beam of light lit up the wooden chest.

'We can hide in there!' cried Wayne. 'Quick!'

Boys are not supposed to scream. They are supposed to grit their teeth and look extra-tough and braver than average. But when Wayne and Craig started clambering into the oak chest they suddenly screamed. Then they clambered out again. Fast.

71

The two screams (one was an *ahh!* and the other an *eeek!*) were just what the dinner ladies wanted to hear.

'They're in there!' hissed Granny Fang.

'In where?' asked Slow.

'In behind this door!'

'Let's get 'em!'

'Blimey, Slow. You aint half thick. Wotcha wanna get 'em for?' whispered Granny.

'We don't really want 'em, Slow,' explained little Batty taking hold of Slow's nose in a friendly way and twisting it.

'Yeth we do!' growled the toothless Sludge. She was in an ultra-savage mood from having to run so fast with a snatcher up her skirt.

'No we don't,' replied little Batty soothingly. 'All we wants to do is to make a getaway—quick—wiv the pink diamond.'

'Who's got it?' asked Slow slowly.

'The snatcher's still got it,' answered Batty breathlessly. 'She aint 'ad no chance to 'and it over—'ave you, my lovely?'

'No,' replied a deeply muffled voice.

'Keep your trap shut! And keep yer 'and in! Old Thrasher's coming!' warned Granny. 'And don't try anything funny!'

'Or else!' said Sludge.

Her narrow skirt had slowed the Thrasher down. Also she had been plunged back into deep despair.

Yes. She'd been really pleased when it had been

proved that the hovering hand was not a figment of her mad mind. That meant she was not mad and would not be sent to the Dunyellin Rest Home. But, as she followed the nuns upstairs, she had seen something too crazy to be true. One of the nuns—the biggest one with the ugliest face—had *four* feet and, presumably, four legs to go with them.

Miss Thrasher's heart had sagged when she saw that. 'I must be mad after all!' she'd thought. 'Maybe I am completely bonkers! Maybe there aren't any nuns! Maybe I'm not running upstairs after them!' Then after a bit, she thought: 'I expect it's all a dream!' After that she slowed down a bit; there's no point in getting puffed out if you're only having a dream. But was it a dream? When she caught up with the nuns they seemed unpleasantly real, smelling strongly of drink and tobacco. You don't get smells in dreams; so it wasn't a dream after all.

'You search in there, an' we'll go on down the corridor,' said the nun with the filed teeth pointing at the BOGWITCH door.

The door crashed open. Two terrified figures charged out.

Thump! That was Wayne's head hitting Mrs Sludge in the tummy.

'Oof!' That's what she said about it as she fell over.

'Caroline!' That's what Craig cried a moment later.

'Run!' Caroline shrieked at him. She needn't have bothered to shriek because Craig was running as fast as

73

ever he could. So was Wayne—bouncing off the Sludge had slowed him down, but he was back on his feet and running.

'Get her! She's got the diamond!' roared Slow in case the other dinner ladies hadn't noticed what was going on.

But they had. They were fully abreast of the situation. And so was Miss Thrasher. The Thrasher's mighty mind worked swiftly on the facts. This is what it had worked out:

1 Those nuns are not nuns.
2 They are dinner ladies.
3 In disguise!
4 They have disguised themselves as nuns by dressing up in nun kits.
5 They have kidnapped Caroline Crisp!
6 They have stolen the pink diamond . . .
7 . . . of Portugal.
8 This means that they are very naughty people.
9 Very, very, very naughty. What they need is . . .
10 . . . a good thrashing!
11 I will give them one.
12 That is my duty.
13 The children are running down the corridor.
14 I will stop the dinner ladies from chasing them.
15 I will stand in the way.
16 They will not dare to hit me.

Tap! That was the Sludge knocking her out with a knapper-tapper.

Bump! That was Miss Thrasher landing in a crumpled heap. (A knapper-tapper is a special burgling cosh for tapping people's heads with—hard.)

It took the dinner ladies about half a minute to hide the Thrasher; then they set off after the children. There was a fire door at the end of the long corridor—the sort that if you barged into it hard, it flew open and you could bound through it to the fire escape. *Clatter, clatter.* Six little feet clattered down the fire escape.

9

Three little hearts thumped and bumped.

'How did you find me?' hissed Caroline as she rushed headlong down the stairs three steps at a time.

'We're detectives!' cried Wayne.

'Ace detectives!' squeaked Craig.

'Yeh! We ....' Wayne wanted to do a bit of boasting about how they'd brilliantly tracked her down and masterminded her escape. But the dinner ladies had arrived at the top of the fire escape; the children could feel the vibrations as Sludge and Co. thundered after them. So Wayne closed his mouth and concentrated on speed.

The children's feet suddenly stopped clattering; grass was under them now as they raced away from the house into the inky night. It was difficult seeing where to go; Craig didn't dare squeeze his torch because he didn't want the dinner ladies to see where they were. Then: *Splash!* Wayne rushed up to his knees into something wet. What could it be? A lake? A river? The moon appeared from behind a dark cloud. Yes—it was water all right—lots of it. And something else too: a boat! There was a rowing boat tied to a post.

'Quick!'

'Get in!'

'Hurry!'

'Untie the rope!'

'Come on!'

Rowing a boat isn't easy because the oars keep coming out of the rowlocks and you keep falling off your seat and landing on the floor. And there's always a terrible, cold, clammy feeling round your bottom when you're sitting on the floor. This terrible, cold, clammy feeling is water seeping into your pants. Then you stand up and everyone shrieks: 'Sit down, you fool! You'll turn the boat over!' So you sit down again on your wet behind and try and get the oars back in place while everyone moans at you and groans at you and screams things like: 'I thought you said you *knew* how to row!' and 'Yeh! You nearly tipped us all into the drink!' and, 'Honestly—my granny can row better 'n you!' Things like that.

So you get a bit peeved and say, 'All right then, if *you're* so clever, let's see if you can do any better!'

Then you pull in the oars and lots of cold water shoots down your sleeves. Then you let go and get up off your seat while they yell, 'Sit down!' That's exactly what happened to Wayne Drain. He told the other two that they could row instead.

So they did—both at once. They sat next to each other and each gripped tightly to an oar.

Splash! Splonk!

'See!' cried Caroline triumphantly.

'You're going round and round in circles!' retorted Wayne.

'No we aren't!'

'Yes you are. Round and round and round.'

'We may be going round and round—but we're *not* going round in circles. We're going round in *oblongs*.'

Then they stopped going round and round and round and round. They stopped dead. It was just as if a huge hand had grabbed them from under the water.

'We've hit something!' cried Wayne.

'What's that noise?'

They could hear a long hissing sigh: the sort a sad elephant might make; it seemed to come from under the boat.

Bonk. Biff. Clonk.

Splashy sorts of bonkings came from under the water jarring and juddering the boat.

The children went very, very quiet. Something strange and dangerous was going on. A strange, dangerous-looking head reared up out of the water and went *WONK!*

Wonk is what sea-lions say when they want some fish, but Craig didn't know that. The wonking head was right next to his and he thought it must be a terrible water-monster out there in the dark going *Wonk* to frighten them. The sea-lion looked at Craig with an eager, expectant face. People didn't usually come onto the lake at night and that meant nights were boring, because people were good fun and had fish. He looked at the small humans hopefully. '*Wonk!*' he went again.

The small humans seemed a bit thick. They just sat

there instead of grabbing a bucket of fish and flinging them round, which is what humans were supposed to do.

The cry of *Wonk* might have struck terror into the hearts of Wayne Drain, Craig Vague, and Caroline Crisp, but it came as a very welcome sound to all the other sea-lions. Yes, that *Wonk* was like an invitation to a midnight feast!

Flop. That was Clarence, the big bull sea-lion belly-flopping into the lake. He swam under water all the way to the boat where he stuck his nose out of the water next to Caroline, breathed at her, and disappeared again.

'*Wonk!*' he barked, joining the first sea-lion.

Craig shone his torch about the boat; curious, whiskered faces blinked in the unexpected light.

'*Wonk!*' said Clarence eagerly.

Using the torch like that was *not* a good idea. The dinner ladies saw it. 'There they are, girls, in a little boat!' gurgled Batty merrily. 'Sludge can swim out and get 'em!'

'I'm not swimming nowhere!' growled the Sludge.

'She don't have to,' hissed Granny Fang, ''cos there's another little boat—look!'

Sure enough, further along the bank, was another rowing boat. Granny had seen it in the dim moonlight as she'd glared this way and that wondering what to do. Now she knew.

'Okay,' she croaked, 'we'll drag it further away and

then we'll row it across real quiet. We'll wait on the other side; soon as they lands—*thump!*'

'Yeh!'

'Yeh!'

'Dur!'

Clarence decided that going *Wonk* was useless. 'These small humans are *too thick* to understand *wonks*,' that's what he thought. 'What they need is *bonks*—that'll wake 'em up!'

BONK!

That was Clarence giving the children's boat an extra-big *bonk*. He just charged at it with his head; it was frightening.

'Look,' cried Caroline, 'we're going to get pushed into that island!'

'Yes,' agreed Craig.

'When we land—jump out quick!' was Wayne's advice.

'Okay.'

'Here they come!' growled Granny Fang.

'Blimey—look at 'em!' sniggered Batty.

The dinner ladies were waiting eagerly on the island, crouching in the undergrowth, peeping out from behind tree trunks.

'Shop it!' grumbled Sludge toothlessly.

'Stop what?'

'Throwing acorns at me. Just shop it!'

Ping!

Thud!

Acorns bounced off Sludge's head.

'Batty!' growled Granny.

''Snot me!' hooted Batty in the special *eerie* voice she had used when she'd been pretending to be the ghost.

'Slow!'

'What?' asked the dur voice of the dim one.

'My God!' gasped Batty. 'Look up there!'

'Blimey,' croaked Granny, looking up into the branches of a tree. 'It's Miss Thrasher!'

'Can't be!'

'Looks like 'er—*OW!*'

'What's she doing up a tree?' asked Slow.

'Why aint she got no clothes on?' asked Batty.

'Whysh she shucking shacorns?'

'How come she's hanging upside down by her feet?' Granny wondered. 'And what's she doing with that stick—scratchin' 'er bottom—how disgusting!'

10

Hanging by your feet from a tree is a deeply wonderful experience, especially in moonlight. It makes you feel in tune with the universe—really happy. That is what Evangeline, the elderly ape, thought. It was Evangeline whom the dinner ladies had seen, not poor Miss Thrasher.

Evangeline scratched herself a bit harder and watched the four strange ladies who had just scrambled ashore onto Monkey Island. 'Humans are really weird,' she thought. 'Fancy dressing up in funny clothes and crouching in the brambles when you could be hanging upside down in a tree scratching your bottom with a stick.'

Splash! Zonk! Splif! Bonk!

'Good grief! More humans! Little ones! Three huddled together in a boat being zonked and bonked by sea-lions. What wild, mad creatures humans are— sea-lions too, come to that.' Evangeline did not approve of sea-lions; sea-lions were always going *Wonk!* and disturbing her deep thoughts. It's hard to be in tune with the universe when idiot sea-lions keep wonking. Evangeline gazed down at the three children and thought how nice they looked in the moonlight— quite like little chimps. Then she frowned. What were those stupid sea-lions trying to do to those sweet, chimp-like children? What were they up to with their bonking and their wonking?

Evangeline stopped scratching her bottom and pulled her lips back over her teeth. This was not a smile. No. It meant she was angry and no longer in tune with the universe. Now what was happening? Those big humans had suddenly leapt out of the brambles and were trying to grab the children. Evangeline's hair started to stand on end—not a good sign. Those stupid sea-lions seemed to be in league with the big humans. It was some sort of evil plan to harm those handsome, chimp-like children. Every time the sea-lions bonked the boat close to the island, the big humans tried to grab them.

Evangeline watched.

Wonk! That was Clarence wonking.

Bonk! That was Clarence bonking.

'Go on Sludge! Get 'em!' That was Granny Fang yelling.

Clunk! That was Craig poking Sludge in the nose with the end of his oar.

Yow! That was Sludge. Apparently she didn't like being poked in the nose with oars. It did not make her feel in tune with the universe.

Evangeline watched as the children madly thrashed with their oars and shoved the boat away from the island. Then: *bonk!* Clarence bonked them right back again.

Fortunately the banks of Monkey Island were very

steep. In fact they were really walls made from tree trunks; they were like that to stop the sea-lions coming ashore and irritating the apes. This meant that the dinner ladies couldn't just paddle into the water and get at the children; they had to lean right over the water and grab at them.

Evangeline watched them doing this; she watched them leaning right over the water. She observed their fat, upturned bottoms as they bent over the bank. Then, very quietly, she climbed down from her tree.

Poor Clarence! Those small humans were *so thick*! He had been wonking and bonking at them to remind them to chuck fish. But had they chucked fish? No. Not so much as a sprat.

Splash!

Splash!

Splash!

More huge splashes. Great! Down went his great head into murky water as he went to get his share.

'Quick!' yelled Wayne Drain. 'Row *properly*—to the other side!' Those unfortunate children did not want to land on the island any more. No fear.

'Did you see that *thing* that pushed the dinner ladies in?' Caroline asked grimly.

'I thought it was Miss Thrasher!' cried Craig.

'No, it was some sort of hideous monster,' said Wayne, 'with a stick.'

'Exactly—Miss Thrasher!'

'No—it was covered in hair . . . .'

Fortunately Evangeline, the elderly ape, did not hear these remarks. She was back up her tree now, upside down again, watching the sea-lions ducking and splurging the big humans. 'Yes,' thought Evangeline, 'pushing them in had been the right thing to do.' She was happy again.

All over Monkey Island other apes were clambering up trees to get a better view. They'd heard the splashing and the shrieking and left their cosy ape house to watch the action. The younger, more frivolous apes got quite excited. They chattered and gibbered merrily, especially when they saw little Batty riding on Clarence's back.

Yes. Clarence was being ridden like a bucking bronco. Sometimes the apes could see most of Clarence as he surged along on the surface; sometimes they could just see Batty's grinning head cutting through the icy water; sometimes they couldn't see anything at all.

It's wonderful how terror stops you being vague. Craig was really rowing keenly, pushing with all his strength.

'You're not supposed to push!' yelled Wayne. 'Pull!'

'Cor,' thought Caroline, 'if Craig's pushing I'd better push my oar too!' So she began to push at the water with her oar just as Craig switched to pulling. They still went round and round in oblongs—but now it was the other way round. It made a nice change.

Evangeline scratched her bottom happily as she watched the children land on the far side of the lake.

The big, bad humans had fought off the sea-lions and were floundering after them but they were a long, long way away. Those chimp-like little humans were going to be all right. Unless . . . .

Evangeline stopped scratching. Her teeth appeared once more. Her hair stood up again. What *were* they doing clambering over that high steel fence? Were those children mad?

11

Back in the banqueting hall, the Cobweb Club was humming and buzzing.

'I have telephoned the police,' announced the professor scratching his beard anxiously, 'and they will be coming round as soon as "Come Dancing" has finished.'

The Cobweb buzz went up a bit and then down again as the bearded one pushed back his glasses and continued: 'I fear something might have happened to Prudence Thrasher and those four brave nuns,' he said gravely. The history teachers nodded. 'Those two delinquent boys may have attacked those defenceless ladies. We must find them at once. Search everywhere!'

That's how it was that, twenty minutes later, the door leading to the bogwitch creaked open. A bearded head popped inside. 'There's no one here,' announced the beard.

'But we've searched all over the house!' cried Sherbet Lemon pushing his way into the room. 'Maybe they're hiding in that box!'

'That's the bogwitch,' explained Watford Smith. 'They wouldn't be in there.' Soon the room was full of history teachers buzzing softly. *Bogwitch, bogwitch, bogwitch* went the buzzing.

'I don't think I've ever seen the bogwitch,' remarked

Sherbet Lemon. 'I'm not very brave I'm afraid. But now that I have had two whole glasses of sherry I think I could stand it.' He pointed his red nose in the direction of the oak chest and began to walk towards it. Even though he had had *two whole* glasses of sherry, he managed to walk quite well; his nose gave off a cheerful glow.

It's strange how eerie, grim, ghostly things can stay eerie, and grim and ghostly even when cheerful things, like red noses, are hovering about. Despite Sherbet's nose, and despite Watford Smith's beard, and despite all the buzzing, the bogwitch chest still looked frightening. It was partly because it stood all by itself in the middle of the room and partly because they knew there was a mummified witch inside it with a terrible grin like a letterbox. Then there was the skinny hand that suddenly appeared over the edge of the chest.

'The bogwitch!' screamed Sherbet.

'Bogwitch!' echoed the Cobweb Club.

All the colour drained away from Sherbet's nose. It was a pale, poetic nose as it pointed at the bogwitch. Sherbet could not take his eyes off that skinny hand; he did not turn and run like the rest of the Cobweb Club, but stayed transfixed watching with fearful, awestruck eyes. The professor felt like running but he forced himself to stay; he'd never seen a ghost before and now he was going to meet one. His hair tingled; sweat ran down his face into his beard. There was a sudden crash as his glasses dropped to the floor. A gasp!

Yes—Sherbet Lemon gasped. Another skinny hand had appeared. It clutched at the other side of the chest. The bogwitch appeared to have extended her mummified, bony arms and was clutching the rim of her chest to pull herself out. The knuckles on that skinny hand stood out white and knobbly. They heard an unearthly groan. It sounded like a groan from someone who had been disturbed after sleeping for thousands of years and didn't like it.

Then Sherbet screamed. He screamed because an evil face suddenly peered at him from over the edge of the chest.

'Bogwitch!' he sobbed as he crumpled to the floor.

The evil face glared at him and opened its evil mouth: 'You drunken fool,' it snapped, 'you've wet your pants!'

This was true. People who see ghosts often wet their pants. It is one of the many things about meeting ghosts that is unpleasant. It is always wise, when visiting a haunted house, to take with you a change of clothes.

'You know what you need, don't you?' hissed the evil face.

'N—no!' stammered Sherbet Lemon.

'A good thrashing!' replied the thing. 'And if I was feeling fit, I'd give you one myself!'

So saying, Miss Thrasher dragged herself out of the chest and staggered about the floor before collapsing into a chair.

'Prudence!' cried Watford Smith as he watched her

collapsing. 'Did those young delinquents do this to you?'

'No,' replied the Thrasher icily. 'They did not!'

'We have got to save those poor children, all *three* of them,' muttered Miss Thrasher grimly when she had explained what had happened. 'They are out there somewhere,' she cried pointing out at the inky night, 'and so are the dinner ladies!'

Watford Smith paced anxiously to the window, opened it and gazed into the darkness. A strange sound wafted in from far away.

'What's that?' asked Miss Thrasher.

'The lions!' he replied softly.

12

The first thing to say about the lion enclosure is that it was very dark. Clouds had come tumbling across the starry sky. Everything was black. But the inkiest part of the enclosure was the deep, dark den where the lions slept.

Yes. It was inky in there—and stinky too! But the lions didn't seem to mind. They liked their deep, cave-like lair because it had a radiator inside to keep them snug. Casper, the biggest, wildest, most ferocious lion, was the one that got to sleep next to the radiator; then a whole heap of lions piled themselves on top of him. Yes, Casper was a very warm lion.

The coldest lion was young Sinbad; he was the one nearest the mouth of the cave; the one that always had either a cold tail or a cold head, depending on which way he turned round. Unfortunately Sinbad's tail was warm that night, which meant that his head was resting on the floor at the mouth of the cave. Now Sinbad's cold ears were attached to his cold head, which is how he heard Caroline gasping.

The cold ears suddenly pricked up alertly. A strange rumbling, grumbling noise came out of his mouth; he bared his teeth rather in the way that Evangeline or Granny Fang did when they were angry. Only Sinbad's teeth were rather more impressive than Evangeline's; they were even more impressive than Granny Fang's.

Caroline had gasped because Wayne had suddenly stopped walking and she'd bumped into him and hurt her nose. It makes your eyes go all watery when that happens. The reason Wayne had stopped was that he had walked into a tree. There had been a dull *clunk,* which had been Wayne's head; then there'd been a dull *thud,* which had been Caroline's nose. Then there'd been the gasp. After that there was roaring. Lots of it.

Lions are very fast runners, as I'm sure you know, and very good leapers. But what they're best at is killing things. Out they tumbled from the inky-stinky, snug fug into the cold, black night. There were strong scents on the winds and sounds of running. Great!

Perhaps it was a mistake to let Sherbet Lemon drive the landrover. But the professor wanted to have both hands free in case he had to use his gun. Miss Thrasher would have been a better driver, despite being wobbly from the knapper-tapper.

'Keep to the track!' yelled the bearded one urgently.

'What track?' asked Sherbet.

'For God's sake, sit down! How can you drive like that!'

But he didn't sit down, you know why. Don't tell anyone.

'Listen!' hissed a grim voice from the back; it was Miss Thrasher. 'You can hear the roaring even over the noise of the engine.'

That was true. The landrover's engine was very loud because Sherbet had forgotten to change out of first gear, but, even so, they could still hear the lions.

'We're too late!' sighed Watford Smith. 'What a terrible way to go—being eaten!'

The three of them peered ahead to where the landrover's headlights sliced through the night.

'Faster!' snapped Miss Thrasher.

'Change gear!' ordered the professor.

There was a juddering and a grinding as Sherbet thrashed about with the gear lever.

'Look where you're going!'

Sherbet stopped trying to change gear and concentrated on looking out of the window. Then: *slam*—he stamped on the brake. The landrover jolted to a stop. None of them spoke. They just stared and felt sick, helpless, and scared. That's how you feel when you see a wild creature with blood on its fangs.

Sinbad felt scared and sick too; it was his blood, you see. Yes. Granny Fang had just sunk her filed fangs into his tail—*thwock!*—then she thwocked him across the backside with her poker. This is not the sort of thing that's supposed to happen to you if you are a lion. It is undignified.

The lions had come out rushing and roaring, you see, and they'd smelt this rich scent of human armpits and evil breath wafting up to them from down by the lake. The moon had popped out from behind the clouds and they'd seen four meaty ladies. Casper had got terribly excited because one of them had looked like a wart-hog and wart-hogs have a nice taste. But two of the meaty ladies were armed with oars from the children's boat.

'Sludge, Slow, grab an oar each. Batty, you grab the boathook. I got me poker down me knickers. We'll get that diamond off those kids. Come on!' That's what Granny Fang had said to them through her chattering teeth as they had stood, wet and shivering, by the edge of the lake.

'They went up over the fence, Granny,' Batty had cackled eagerly.

'Right then, so shall we.'

Sludge had been the first to realise that they'd broken into the lion enclosure. 'Listen!' she'd cried. 'Bloomin' lions!' Then Casper had come rushing out of the night eager for a mouthful of wart-hog.

That's when the fighting started. The four damp dinner ladies stood back-to-back wielding their heavy weapons while the lions stalked round them in a ring. Sometimes one would rush in at them and then—*clunk!* An oar would flash out, wielded by the mighty Sludge and the whacked lion would slink back to the others.

'I wish it weren't so dark,' muttered Granny, 'you can't 'ardly see 'em till they're almost on top of you.'

'Well, what we gonna do then?' asked Sludge.

'Get eaten I expect,' gurgled Batty in her usual merry way.

'Well, why are you so cheerful then?' the

Sludge grunted.

'Gotta look on the bright side,' Batty sniggered.

'What bright side?'

'We'll save money—no funeral!' squawked Batty. 'We'll be all ate up!'

''Ere, I 'ope those kids 'ave bin et!' said the dur voice of Slow.

''Course they 'ave!'

'I do 'ope so. I do. I could die 'appy if I knew they was all et up!'

But Slow did not die happy. No. She did not die at all.

Suddenly headlamps blinded their eyes; a *bang* shook them and made their ears go funny.

Voices.

'Good grief!' one of the voices shrieked. 'It's the dinner ladies!'

'Blimey,' growled Granny, 'old Ma Thrasher. What's she doing? Trying to shoot us?'

'Prudence!' yelled another voice. 'Stay inside!'

'I will *not*,' replied Miss Thrasher firmly. 'I'm going to see what's happened to those children!'

Evangeline, the elderly ape, scratched her bottom sadly. She could see the lights of the landrover and the police cars that were joining it. Together the headlights made a shining pool of light in the darkness. She heard more loud bangs—the professor shooting into the air— and roaring as the lions slunk back to their lair.

The agitated ape was looking for signs of the three chimp-like children, but she could only see grown-ups: the professor, Sherbet Lemon, Miss Thrasher, the dinner ladies, and the police ballroom dance display team looking spruce and glamorous. Evangeline stopped scratching. She started to gibber—an excited, bubbling sound: she'd seen something that had made her deeply in tune with the universe.

Yes—one of those little chimp-like chaps—she was sure of it—up a tree—hanging upside down.

It was Wayne. He was hanging upside down in order to help Caroline; he was lowering her down the tree; he lowered and lowered as far as he could; then he let go. She fell onto something soft: young Craig Vague. 'Umph!'

It was nice in the back of the landrover, even though the Thrasher was in there saying things like, 'We must get you straight home to bed. It'll be school in the morning!'

None of them minded. No. It was just nice being alive and warm and safe with Professor Watford Smith driving them home.

'I wonder if the police will catch the dinner ladies?' asked Craig.

'Shouldn't think so!' laughed Wayne.

'Still at least they won't be coming back to *our* school!'

This was true. The dinner ladies never returned to

the Littlesprat Primary School. They got away though—and now they are lying low again.

Look very carefully at *your* dinner ladies; if one of them has filed teeth and one of them looks like a wart-hog and one of them is far thicker than average and one of them is bats—then don't eat the rice!

THE HEADMASTER WENT SPLAT!

David Tinkler

'Kevin Twerp,' hissed Killer Keast, the ferocious headmaster of Shambles School, 'I want to see you in my room immediately.'

Suddenly, it seemed to go cold. The light went dim. There was a gasp from the children and the teachers shivered. Kevin felt faint and his mouth went dry.

Kevin Twerp's life hasn't been easy; pop-singing dad killed in an air crash, Mum – Nitty Norah the Hair Explorer – driven out to work as a school nurse. And, looming, like a dark shadow, Killer Keast.

But, with the help of WPC Rose Button, lodger and All-England Mud Wallowing Champion, things *will* change . . .!

KNIGHT BOOKS

MY RECORD BOOK

Gyles Brandreth

The pogo bouncing, baked bean picking, wellie-wanging, jolly jelly record book!

How many pairs of socks can *you* put on, one on top of another? Can *you* eat an entire tin of baked beans in 19 minutes using only a cocktail stick? And what exactly *are* the credentials for being a record-breaker?

YOU'D BETTER GET A COPY AT RECORD SPEED AND FIND OUT!

KNIGHT BOOKS

DIRTY, LOUD AND BRILLIANT

Carol Vorderman

Bet you can't
* hold a cup with one finger
* light a torch with a lemon
* make a table top hovercraft
With DIRTY, LOUD AND BRILLIANT – you can!

Masses of easy-to-follow mind-boggling experiments using stuff you'll find at home.

Have a Dirty, Loud and Brilliant time!

KNIGHT BOOKS

THE REAL GHOSTBUSTERS™

JANINE'S GENIE

Novelisation by Kenneth Harper

The Real Ghostbusters have arrived, and they're the hottest, spook-hunting brains on the streets. Four brave men, one daring woman, and one crazy lump of ectoplasm set on a mission of high-class ghost-trapping – where no spirit has a ghost of a chance!

When a client offers the Ghostbusters the pick of his belongings instead of payment, Janine chooses a ridiculous, old brass oil-lamp and unleashes a load of trouble on to town!

THE REAL GHOSTBUSTERS – They're here to save the world!

KNIGHT BOOKS

A CATALOGUE OF COMIC VERSE

Collected and illustrated by Rolf Harris

A cattle dog (as they say in Australia!) jam-packed with great poems on a variety of different topics – including cats and dogs – to say nothing of tigers and terrified tortoises, some rather curious eating habits and some loony relations.

This rumbustious collection for children of all ages has been compiled and interpreted with wittily refreshing drawings by Rolf Harris, author of the best-selling *Your Cartoon Time*, and favourite of children everywhere.

KNIGHT BOOKS